GW00870171

Love

Lottie
x

This Book Belongs To

_____

For my Grandchildren Oscar, Fergus and Belle
Who inspired me to write about our pets.

Published in the United Kingdom by:

Blue Falcon Publishing
The Mill, Pury Hill Business Park,
Alderton Road, Towcester
Northamptonshire NN12 7LS
Email: books@bluefalconpublishing.co.uk
Web: www.bluefalconpublishing.co.uk

A CIP record of this book is available from the British Library.

First printed September 2021
ISBN 9781912765423

Archie

and the

Chickens

Lottie Loake

Archie is a little cat, with a very stripy coat and a long tail. He looks just like a tiger.

He lives with his sister Millie, who has lots of spots like a leopard,

a big black dog called Eric,

and three garden chickens.

"Morning, Millie! Morning, Eric! What a lovely day it is today," says Archie as he puts his head out of the door. He looks around the sunny garden and lets out a happy "Meow!"

"MEOW"

Archie does a hop, a skip and a jump and races outside,

leaping up onto a tall garden fence.

With his tail in the air and a smile on his face. Archie watches the chickens wander up the garden, chatting noisily to each other.

Millie and Eric see Archie on the fence. "Oh no!" whispers Millie to Eric.
"I don't like the way Archie is looking at the chickens, with his tail swishing like that.
He's up to something! We all know how much he likes to surprise them."

Archie's bottom goes in the air, his tail waves from side to side and he pounces towards the chickens.

Eric and Millie watch in horror as Archie lands in a roly-poly right in the middle of the chickens.

Dolly, Molly and Sophie get such a scare and, with lots of clucking and feathers flying, they run in all directions.

Dolly jumps on to a wooden bench.

Molly hides under the garden table.

Poor Sophie ends up in Eric's paddling pool with a big splash!

When they look at Archie he is rolling around on the grass,
laughing so hard there are tears in his eyes.

"Ha Ha!

Ha Ha!"

Sophie, Dolly and Molly are very cross, and they chase Archie around the garden shouting,

Archie is too fast for them and races away, grinning.

"We need to teach Archie a lesson!" Dolly says to Sophie and Molly. "We should give him a fright!" Sophie replies crossly as she shakes out her wet feathers.

So, the chickens hide behind a tree, waiting for Archie to walk by.

Archie wanders back up the garden, looking very pleased with himself.
"Ha, ha-ha," he chuckles. "Scaring the chickens today was really funny."

"Ha, ha-ha!"

Suddenly, from behind the tree, out jump, Dolly, Molly and Sophie.

Archie gets such a shock that he bounces up into the air and runs back into the house with his tail between his legs.

"MEOW"

"Archie won't be scaring us again," laugh the chickens as they stroll away puffing out their feathers.

Poor Archie. I think he has learnt his lesson today.
He won't be frightening the chickens anymore.

THE END

Just For Fun!

How many chickens are missing from the picture?

Just For Fun!

Who is missing from the paddling pool?

Just For Fun!

Who is missing from under the table?

Lightning Source UK Ltd.
Milton Keynes UK
UKHW051918210921
390962UK00002B/44